THE CONQUERED SITS AT
THE BUS STOP, WAITING

# THE CONQUERED SITS AT THE BUS STOP, WAITING

VERONICA
MONTES

STORIES

Black
Lawrence
Press

Black
Lawrence
Press

www.blacklawrence.com

Executive Editor: Diane Goettel
Chapbook Editor: Kit Frick
Book and Cover Design: Amy Freels
Cover Art: "The Young House" by Mary Jhun. Used with permission.

Published 2020 by Black Lawrence Press.
Printed in the United States.

For Drew, Risa, Vida, and Lea,
who were with me
and all around me
as I wrote.

# Contents

# The Conquered Sits at the Bus Stop, Waiting

She chooses a red stone, places it on the center of her tongue, sucks gently. Her toes are covered in dust. She was young once, tender-skinned and lush, the whole of her like a forest. The men came one after another, circumnavigating the expanse of her body, licking its contours, extracting gold. Her hair sprung from her head like coils, but all that remains now are tight whorls of black set like punctuation marks along her scalp. When you call out, she will cover her eyes as if you are made of sunlight.

# The Sound of Her Voice

It happens when she speaks. Her husband's face disassembles itself, and the pieces do not slide back into their proper slots until she stops making sounds. Sometimes she forgets and a single word escapes her—a word like *no* or *when*—and her husband's left eye migrates to the right side of his forehead for a moment. She cannot bear to see him out of sorts in this way.

It's her fault. Her side of the conversation was always filled with pauses because she could never seem to find the right words, and so she would backtrack and come at it in a different way, a way she felt might be better, or might better express, maybe, the point she was trying to make. Her husband once mentioned that he didn't like this, that her tendency to speak in spirals was maddening. *You're driving me fucking nuts*, he said.

She makes use of gestures now. There is a whole language, after all, that incorporates fingerspelling and body motion. She's consulted a website that claims this language can improve relationships. Also—did you know this?—gestures are an effective way to speak with babies who don't yet vocalize. She keeps this in mind for the future.

Maybe she'll take a class in this language. For now, though, she wings it *(holds arms out to the side, tilts body to the left, then the right)*. Near dinnertime she raises both hands, fingers spread, so that her husband knows his meal will be ready in ten minutes. Later, when he's settled onto the couch to watch television, she cups her hand around her ear to ask if he'd like the volume turned up. Sometimes a raised eyebrow is enough to telegraph her message, and she's found that there are many different ways to nod even though they all mean *yes*. He seems grateful for this silence; he sighs as if content.

In bed tonight she places her cheek over her husband's heart to indicate that she'd welcome intimacy. She's surprised to find that his heartbeat feels like a tiny punch, punch, punch against her face. It makes her laugh (to herself). Afterward there is a rustling outside the window, and she knows that it's the two deer who come to feed off the apple tree at midnight.

*Can you hear*— she begins.

He strokes her hair. He places his hand over her mouth. *Shhhh*, he says. *Shhhh*.

# Lint Trap

After she moves a load of warm laundry from the dryer to the folding basket for the fourth time that morning, she gathers the detritus of her family's T-shirts and socks from the lint trap. She wonders (also for the fourth time that morning) if there isn't something to be done with the lint itself. She fingers the fluff of it. Could she use it to ... stuff something? A tiny doll family? Tooth fairy pillows? She sneezes.

When she was a child in Oregon, her mother sent her to a school where they spent all day dancing and painting and rolling sheets of beeswax into tapers. In the third grade, they were given tufts of colored wool, which they repeatedly stabbed with a needle until the fibers locked together and became a sort of sculpting material. She was never very good at this. She often pricked herself by accident and then braced for blood that mysteriously failed to appear. The other children bent their heads to their task and produced gnomes and fairies, elephants and foxes. She made balls of various sizes. That's it: balls.

She recalls a news segment featuring a frugal couple who busied themselves by transforming plastic grocery bags into area rugs. *Was* it area rugs? Or curtains? She considers the possibility of using the lint from the dryer to create kneepads and headbands to protect her four children—or wait, yes, *all* children!—from the dangers of asphalt and ceramic tile. She envisions wild success in the money-making arena of youth sports. What if she became celebrated for halting the outrageous uptick in childhood-sustained concussions? *Concussions, kidcussions, KID-CUSHIONS*, she thinks with satisfaction, wondering if she should have gone into marketing instead of laundry.

And if she does this, will her story go viral, everyone marveling at her domestic ingenuity? Will the lint fill up the space near her solar plexus, where she once carried warm thoughts of her husband? Could she fashion it into something flirty and beguiling to turn his head or, really, anybody's head? Could she prop herself against it to remain alert from three to five in the afternoon? Could she use it to plump the lines that have formed on either side of her mouth or to refill her once magnificent breasts? To muffle her screams, to plug her ears, to cushion her long and graceless fall ...

# Madaling Araw

She awoke, unsurprised, on a bed of crushed glass. Once it was fire ants, once it was lengths of twisted wire, rotting fish, bludgeoned rodents. *They were always doing shit like this.*

She rose to her feet quickly in a single motion and walked into the lake to rinse away the shards semi-buried in her back, her buttocks, her calves. Her hair, like her mother's before her, was thick as twisted rope, and the back of it glittered with sharp bits. The tamsi birds called to each other as she shook it out, excited by the way the glass arced through the air, catching sunlight along the way.

The cold water numbed her discomfort, but she needed something to fend off the pain that would follow. She thought for a moment, then waded to the shore to search for the bush her mother had called tsaang gubat. She bit and squeezed the leaves gently to release their oil, then rubbed them over the cuts that stippled her body. Small welts rose to the surface, like weeds after a rainfall.

When she was done she whispered a thank you to her mother, who had been dead for many years now. She didn't dress for a while, choosing instead to admire her own brown skin, the knots of muscle, every scar and scab. When she was done she turned to the east to face them. *Do you see,* she thought as she held her arms above her head and rotated slowly. *Do you see me standing here?*

From miles away, they saw. Their pale hands flexed, their hearts thrummed with the knowledge of their wrongdoing. When she spat at them, their heads snapped back in unison. Each looked sideways at the other, ashamed of having flinched.

She turned away then and began to walk toward the west, wondering what they would do tomorrow and the next day and the one after that. Blood trickled down between her shoulder blades, where she had not been able to reach.

## Interlude:
## The Ocean of Tears

When her father died, she began to cry and couldn't stop. Under the circumstances it was nothing out of the ordinary, but then several days passed, and still nothing had changed. Every night she fell asleep crying and found, upon waking, that her pillow was soaked through.

She ate her breakfast, brushed her hair and teeth, and dressed while the tears gathered in the corners of her eyes. When she moved her head just so, they spilled onto the collar of her shirt.

On her way to work, other people would catch sight of her in her car, and their pity washed over her in great waves. *It's okay*, she wanted to say. *I'm okay.*

Soon her eyes became mere slits, and tiny bumps formed on the lids. She went to the optometrist, who chided her. "What is going on?" he asked. "What is this all about?" He had flat cheeks and taut skin and, despite being older than her father had been, moved like a much younger man. A knot of resentment lodged in her heart.

"I'm not sure; I think it's because I can't stop crying," she explained. "My father died, and I've been crying and crying."

"Well, that would do it," he said. He shone a flashlight in her eyes and moved it up and down and side to side while making small sounds of disapproval. She waited for him to express polite sorrow over the loss of her father, but he never did.

One night, after many months, a lady appeared in her dreams. She had a tail, much like a mermaid, but there was no water in sight. Instead, she floated from side to side as if navigating currents of air.

"Do you have wings?"

"Wings?" asked the floating mermaid lady. "Why would I have wings?"

"I don't know," she said. There was so much she didn't understand.

The lady pursed her lips and waved her hands about as if to erase the words they'd just exchanged. She began again. "What you must do," she said, "is cry an ocean's worth of tears. Then you must cross that ocean in a boat of your own making. When you reach the other side, you'll find a door. Open it, and this will be finished."

"What will be finished?"

"Your grief, your sadness."

It was easy to cry an ocean's worth of tears, but building the boat proved difficult. Her eyes were nearly swollen shut by then, and there was no one to ask for help. At first, her excessive tears had brought friends rushing to her side. They patted her back; they kissed her head; sometimes they fed her. But now they were gone; it was too much. *She* was too much.

A group of small boys found her one day as she sat in the middle of a mound of wood and nails and tools. At first they laughed and threw tiny

acorns softly at her head, but they eventually tired of their own wicked-
ness and began to help her. When it seemed they might take over, she said,
"Remember, it has to be a boat of my own making."

"All right, all right," they scowled. And they told her to do this and that;
they yelled at her when she hammered their small fingers; they guided
her hands. She waited for them to ask why she was crying, but they were
too busy at their task.

When it was done, the boys pushed her and the boat out into the Ocean
of Tears. They threw tiny acorns softly at her head again until she was too
far away to hit. "Goodbye," they screamed over the ocean. "Goodbye!"
She found they had packed sandwiches for her, and for a few moments
this increased the volume of her tears.

Who knows how long she sailed. What does it matter?

One morning she awoke to find that the boat had drifted ashore and
there, at the far end of the beach, stood a door constructed of weathered
planks. It was just as the lady had promised. When she stepped onto the
sand, her legs, astounded by the sudden call to action, collapsed beneath
her. She thought of her father and how proud he would be to see how far
she'd come in the boat of her own making, and she determined not to
give up.

She dried her tears as best she could, gathered her strength, and began
to use her arms to drag herself toward the door. Halfway there she felt
her legs come to life, and so she stood and walked the rest of the way. The
floating mermaid lady's voice was in her ear all the while: *your grief, your
sadness, will be finished.*

*Open the door.*

The planks were warped, but smooth to the touch, and sun-warmed and beautiful. She gently pressed her hands and forehead against them. Her tears stopped immediately, and she knew the lady had told the truth: all she had to do was push it open. She imagined herself unfurling like an orchid; she imagined becoming herself again.

*Open the door.*

But she couldn't. She lifted her head and pulled her hands away from the smooth wood. She walked back the way she'd come. By the time she pushed the boat away from the shore and climbed in, the crying had begun again in earnest. It took her hours or maybe days or weeks to cross back over the Ocean of Tears. She arrived home at night, tunneled into bed, and cried until she fell asleep. It was like that for many years; it was like that forever.

# The Man Who Came from an Island Where Everyone Knows How to Sing

When I touched him that first time, it was by accident. The second time was on purpose. I left scratches in my wake, and the scent of toasted almonds rose snakelike from the wounds. Intrigued, I bit into the tender flesh at the base of his throat. He tasted of crushed sesame, sweet crab meat, bits of cassia bark. He slapped me lightly across the mouth.

This is when things could have gone one way, but went another.

*I'm sorry*, he said. I licked his tears to stop them, and they were honeyed and sharp like li hing mui. Later, as we fell asleep in his apartment, I wondered if I should tell anyone that I'd found him. This scratch-and-sniff boy, this all-you-can-eat buffet boy.

Of course I told. I told everyone. By the end of May, he had wandered into the soft arms of my friends, into their supplicating palms and bright, searching mouths. I have since learned to hide my secrets, but I can't find one, now, worth keeping.

# The 38 Geary Express

*I have been watching you have you noticed do you like it.* He wrote this in a letter, but she handed it back to him without breaking the seal. First she said, "I don't know you." And then, "Please leave me alone," and also, "I have a boyfriend."

As if those words might have some bearing on what he chose to do with her, as if they would stop him from slipping into the seat behind her on the bus to catch the scent of soap off her neck. He stares now at her long ponytail, fastened at the crown of her head and spilling like ink past her neck. At one point she flips it over the back of her seat, and it nearly reaches his knees. He wants to touch it, pull it, cut it. Paralyzed by his options, he does nothing.

She stands up as the bus jerks towards Balboa Street, steady on her feet, the seat of her jeans tight across her ass. He doesn't bother to move yet because Balboa is not her stop; she has never stopped at Balboa. She wraps her hand around the pole, shifts her weight from her right foot to her left, her hips like an invitation.

At the ATM on Eighth Avenue, she withdraws a twenty-dollar bill, folds it precisely in half, and walks across the street to KFC for something to eat. He always waits outside during this part because he has seen her chew food, and he doesn't enjoy it. He leans against someone's Honda, accidentally setting off the alarm. This bothers no one—not the old Chinese ladies with their pink plastic bags, not the little kids in their windbreakers and light-up shoes, not the men on their phones. He moves confidently to the next car, careful not to make the same mistake.

By the time the two o'clock church bells ring at Star of the Sea, she has finished her lunch. She'll walk to Sixth Avenue, then, and check her phone while she waits for the light to tell her it's safe to cross. He knows where she lives.

# Ruby

Undeterred by the presence of her mother on the opposite side of the room, Ruby is nearly sitting in the boy's lap. Together they flip slowly through an issue of *Vogue* and pretend, for the sake of decorum, that they are admiring the severe beauty of the models. What they're really doing is pointing out words. He points to *wet*; she points to *hard*. He finds the word *stroke*, and she runs her finger across *shaft*. The heat generated between their sixteen-year-old bodies threatens to set the house ablaze.

The boy adjusts the way he's sitting; his breath turns ragged in Ruby's ear. She is repulsed and delighted, just barely grasping at the truth of what's happening. It goes on and on like this, until soon even the most benign words—words like *blush* or *juice*, *melt* or *under*—come alive, pulsing and leaping off the page they're printed on. Ruby's mother looks up from the computer, eyebrows raised, mouth quirked to one side.

"Oh!" the boy says. He jumps from the couch and shoves his hands in his pockets. "I think I left my phone in my car."

"Did you?" says Ruby's mother, already sure that he did not. She knew from the moment he stepped across the threshold that it would come to this. He has the profile of an Aztec god; he is sloe-eyed and broad through the shoulders. Ruby's mother remembers boys like this: the phone calls at midnight, the musk of them.

"I'll help you find it!" Ruby offers.

They stumble out the front door, puppy chasing puppy, and that is the last time that Ruby's mother sees her because Ruby never comes back, not really. The girl who returns to the house is another creature altogether, blind and groping and fettered to an enormous, feral love.

# Acknowledgments

Thank you to the editors of the journals where these stories first appeared:

A version of "The Conquered Sits at the Bus Stop, Waiting" first appeared in *Achiote Seeds*. It was inspired by Bino A. Realuyo's poem "GI Baby" and had as its opening sentence a line from that work.

"The Sound of Her Voice" first appeared in *CHEAP POP*.

"Lint Trap" first appeared in *Lost Balloon*.

"Madaling Araw" first appeared in *Lakas Zine*.

"The Man Who Came from an Island Where Everyone Knows How to Sing" first appeared in *Spelk Fiction*.

A version of "The 38 Geary Express" first appeared in *Achiote Seeds*.

"Ruby" first appeared in *SmokeLong Quarterly*.

Photo: Martin Delfino

Veronica Montes was born in San Francisco and raised in the Filipino American enclave of Daly City, California. Her short stories have appeared in print journals such as *Bamboo Ridge* and *Prism International*, as well as in many anthologies including *Contemporary Fiction by Filipinos in America*, *Growing Up Filipino*, and *Going Home to a Landscape: Writings by Filipinas*. Her flash fiction appears online in various journals including *Wigleaf*, *SmokeLong Quarterly*, *Cheap Pop*, and *Lost Balloon*, among others. She is the author of *Benedicta Takes Wing & Other Stories* (Philippine American Literary House, 2018).